Kathryn Heling and Deborah Hembrook

Clothesline Clues to the First Day of School

Illustrated by Andy Robert Davies

Charlesbridge

Pic
J
Heling
main

With thanks to teachers everywhere, and to all who make school a welcoming place for children!—K. E. H.

For Claire . . . an amazing teacher and friend!—D. K. H.

For my niece, Amy.—A. R. D.

Published by Charlesbridge, 85 Main Street, Watertown, MA 02472
(617) 926-0329 • www.charlesbridge.com

Library of Congress Cataloging-in-Publication Data
Names: Heling, Kathryn, author. | Hembrook, Deborah, author. | Davies, Andy Robert, illustrator.
Title: Clothesline clues to the first day of school / Kathryn Heling and Deborah Hembrook; illustrated by Andy Robert Davies.
Description: Watertown, MA: Charlesbridge, [2019] | Audience: Ages 3-7.
Identifiers: LCCN 2018031379 (print) | LCCN 2018034160 (ebook) | ISBN 9781632897138 (ebook) | ISBN 9781632897145 (ebook pdf) | ISBN 9781580898249 (reinforced for library use) | ISBN 9781580895798 (softcover)
Subjects: LCSH: First day of school — Juvenile literature. | Schools — Juvenile literature. | Clothing and dress — Juvenile literature.
Classification: LCC LB1556 (ebook) | LCC LB1556 .H45 2019 (print) | DDC 371.002l — dc23
LC record available at https://lccn.loc.gov/2018031379

Printed in China
(hc)10 9 8 7 6 5 4 3 2 1
(sc)10 9 8 7 6 5 4 3 2 1

Illustrations done in pencil and mixed media, manipulated digitally
Display type and text type set in Jesterday
Color separations by Colourscan Print Co Pte Ltd, Singapore
Printed by 1010 Printing International Limited in Huizhou, Guangdong, China
Production supervision by Brian G. Walker
Designed by Susan Mallory Sherman, Whitney Leader-Picone, and Sarah Richards Taylor

High on the clotheslines
hang clue after clue.
It's the first day of school!
Who wants to meet you?

STOP

Raincoat and warm gloves,
a hat and stop sign, too.
Safety vest and badge.
Who wants to meet you?

STOP

Your crossing guard!

Book bag and new shirt,
a class roster to review.
Bow tie and jacket.
Who wants to meet you?

Parker
Amy
Julisa
Win-Thi
Sarah
Antonio
Teresa

Your teacher!

Oven mitt, food chart,
a lunch tray or two.
Apron and hairnet.
Who wants to meet you?

Menu
SPAGHETTI
BOLOGNESE
+
FRUIT
SALAD

Your cafeteria cook!

Uniform and key ring.
Recycling to sort through.
Mop, soap, and dustcloth.
Who wants to meet you?

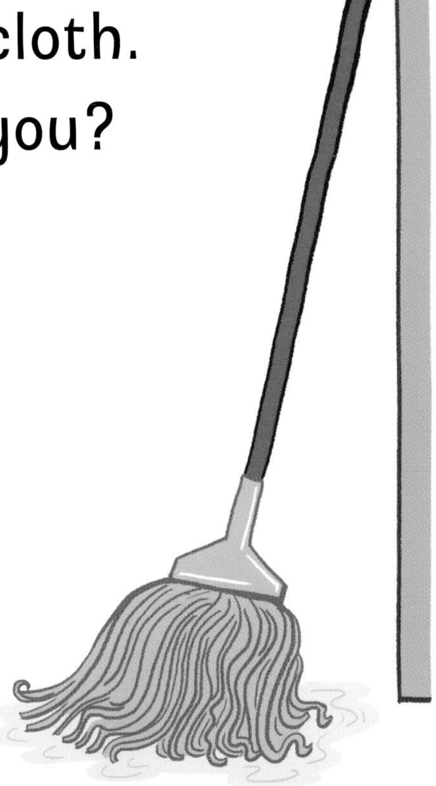

Julisa
Amy
Da'Kye
MOP
SOAP

Your custodian!

Shorts, T-shirt, and socks.
Sneakers, spiffy and new.
Whistle, towel, and clipboard.
Who wants to meet you?

Your gym teacher!

Color wheel and easel,
a painter's smock in blue.
Aprons for everyone.
Who wants to meet you?

Your art teacher!

Pants, shirts, and dresses
in every size and hue.
Coats, scarves, and backpacks.
Who wants to meet you?

Your new friends!

STOP

Each clothesline holds clues
to friends old and new.
On the first day of school,
who welcomes you?